the famine

THE TRAPPS FAMILY ADVENTURES

the famine

By LAWRENCE E.R. ADAMS

Illustrations by ROBERT G. ADAMS

TRAPPS PUBLISHING

First Printed in 2009
Printed in Canada

THE PUBLISHER:
Trapps Publishing
P.O. Box 212
Irricana, Alberta, Canada T0M 1B0

Manufactured by Friesens Corporation in Altona, Canada
October 2009
Job # 50423

Library and Archives Canada Cataloguing in Publication

Adams, Lawrence E. R. (Lawrence Edward Roy), 1941-
The famine / by Lawrence E.R. Adams ; illustrations by Robert G. Adams.

(The Trapps family adventures)
Includes index.
ISBN 978-0-9781533-0-4

1. Inuit--Canada--Juvenile fiction. 2. Inuit mythology--Juvenile fiction.
I. Title. II. Series:°Adams, Lawrence E. R. (Lawrence Edward Roy), 1941- .
Trapps family adventures.

PS8601.D454F35 2009 jC813'.6 C2009-905681-X

Cover: Robert G. Adams

DISCLAIMER

All the characters in this book are fictitious, any similarity between any living or deceased person is merely a coincidence.

<u>AWARDS</u>

"THE OLD ONE," the first book in, **"THE TRAPPS FAMILY ADVENTURES,"** series, was awarded the silver medal for Canada-West-Best Regional Fiction at the 12th Annual Independent Publisher Book Awards in Los Angeles on 30th May 2008.

For my son-in-law TJ and daughter-in-law Coleen

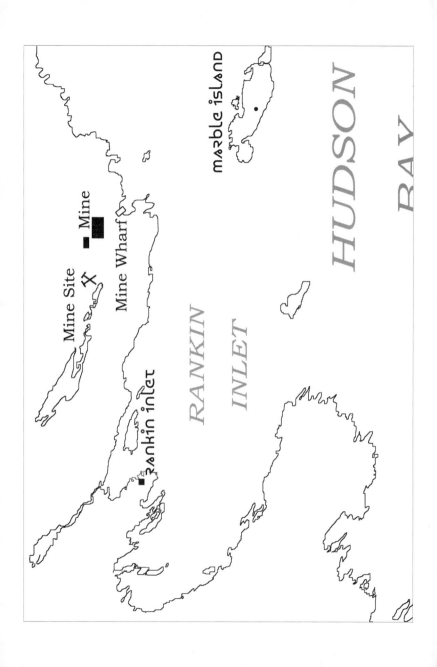

Mine Site

Mine

Mine Wharf

ᕆᐊᓐᑭᓐ ᐃᓐᓚᑦ

Rankin Inlet

RANKIN

INLET

ᒫᕐᐳᓪ ᐃᔅᓚᓐᑦ

marble island

HUDSON

BAY

CONTENTS

PROLOGUE 11

PROLOGUE

It wasn't the call of the North that brought the Trapps family to the vast treeless region of Canada's North, known as the Tundra. This trip had nothing to do with the romance that "the call of the North" evoked; this wasn't even going to be a holiday. Numerous hours of backbreaking work would dominate the expedition, or so they thought.

Max Trapps, a world-class archaeologist, has led expeditions to numerous places in the world conducting excavations to uncover the secrets of the past. He has been chosen to conduct an archaeological dig at an ancient Inuit settlement. Workers at the Blue Diamond Mine, approximately thirty kilometres northeast of Rankin Inlet on the west shore of the Hudson Bay in the Northwest Territories, made the discovery while working near their airstrip. For the duration of the dig, the mining company is generously supplying the food and lodgings for the entire Trapps Family.

When Amy and her brothers, Ty and Parker, meet "THE OLD ONE," the secrets and mysteries of the North and the Inuit way of life will be laid bare before them. Nothing the kids might have done before they left their home in Calgary could have prepared them for the adventures they are about to experience. They are entering an environment that few people have ever seen and fewer will ever live in. It is a harsh and unforgiving land that holds untold beauty, mystery, and adventure for those who dare to accept its challenges. The North is home for the Inuit, the only race of humans who are able to live under its conditions without assistance from the outside world. The Inuit's ability to adapt to their environment allows them to reap the bounty of the North. Only the most adventurous and well-equipped explorers have been able to penetrate the Inuit's habitat and live to tell about it.

Amy's curiosity and her thirst for knowledge sometimes get her into jams that requires the help of her brothers to resolve. She enjoys assisting her father during excavations and likes nothing better than discovering a relic from the past and unlocking its secrets. Ty is twelve, one year younger than Amy, and a gifted athlete. His favorite sport is hockey and if he were allowed, he would play it twenty-four hours a day. Parker, who is one year younger than Ty, doesn't possess his brother's athletic abilities, but his determination to succeed and to not be outdone by anyone makes him a worthy opponent. He possesses a photographic memory, which has proven to be an asset when his sister gets them involved in one of her many schemes.

After meeting the shaman Kadluk (the adults know him as THE OLD ONE) the kids now have the ability to communicate through their Inuas, a gift that is only bestowed upon a shaman. An Inua is the spiritual occupant (spirit helper) that resides in all living and inanimate things.

Kadluk opened a world to the kids they never knew existed. But when they discovered at the dig the first amulet that had been made by the first shaman they learned they were protected in a manner mortal man has only been able to dream. The amulet gives them protection from anything that would otherwise harm them and allows them to approach and travel with dangerous animals.

Chapter 1

AT THE BREAK OF DAWN

Sunday, 29 September, 1985
Dear diary,

It was the strangest feeling I've ever had. I knew something was wrong. I just didn't' know what it was or how serious it would be…

Amy

As Amy looked out her bedroom window she knew there would be no shadows cast on this moonless night. The shadows that appear and disappear at will inspire some and yet drives others mad as they race away only to reappear and play upon one's mind.

14

After a restless night and long before the sun would appear Amy's feet hit the floor. Amy had the feeling something was wrong, but why she didn't know. It was just something she felt. As she emerged from her bedroom she was met by her dad and Parker.

"Where's Ty?" Amy asked.

"He couldn't wait for us. He was too hungry, so he went to the kitchen," Parker replied.

"Is everything okay?" Amy wanted to know.

"Yes. Why do you ask?" Max responded, as he looked at Amy with a questioning look on his face.

"It's nothing, Dad," Amy cheerfully replied as she forced a smile.

Parker speaks to Amy through his Inua.

"Before Ty left he asked me if something was wrong. He said he had a funny feeling that something wasn't right, but he didn't know what it was," Parker advised Amy.

"I've had a strange feeling since I woke up something is wrong but I don't know what it is. I can't shake it and it bothered me so much I didn't get a good sleep," Amy informed Parker.

"I feel the same way, but nothing is wrong that I know of," replied Parker.

15

"Dad, Parker and I will run ahead to the kitchen before Ty eats everything," Amy said with laughter in her voice as she headed for the door. "Come on, Parker, let's go," shouted Amy.

They found Ty sitting alone at a table. The furrows on his brow indicated he was deep in thought.

"What's troubling you this morning? You look like you're a million miles away. I thought you were so hungry you couldn't wait to eat," Amy said to Ty.

"I am, but the cooks haven't put the food out yet," Ty replied pointing to the serving counter.

"Why haven't they?" queried Parker.

"I don't know! I asked the cooks' Inuas and they didn't make any sense. They said the cooks couldn't get to the supplies for some reason. I've been waiting for Mr. Munro to come in and straighten this mess out. I sure hope he hurries up, I'm starving," Ty howled.

"Jiminy-Willie-Peppers, I was just hungry before but now that breakfast isn't ready I'm starving!" wailed Parker as he looked around the kitchen.

"It's okay, Parker," Amy reassured her little brother, "Mr. Munro will straighten everything out when he gets here."

16

"Why isn't he here? He usually beats us to the kitchen in the morning," Ty quipped.

"Well he better hurry up. I'm getting hungrier by the minute," Parker said to no one in particular.

"Come! Hurry! You're needed right away!" the kids heard a voice say through their Inuas.

"Is that you, Kadluk?" cried Amy.

There was no reply. The silence was only broken by the empty void ringing in their ears.

"What do you suppose that means?" Ty's query echoed in the hollow void.

"Jiminy-Willie-Peppers, I'll bet we're going on another journey!" shouted Parker.

a problem is brewing

"**We** must hurry, we haven't got much time," said the Inuit, who was carving a wooden mask.

"Who are you?" Amy inquired; she knew he was a shaman because they were conversing through their Inuas.

"I am Tagak," answered the Inuit, "The Old One told me you and your brothers are powerful shamans so I sent my spirit helpers to find you. We haven't got

18

much time. The People are starving. I have appealed to the lesser spirits and tried to appease them but they will not hear me. Sedna must be very angry; I believe some serious transgressions have been made. Sedna will not let the animals loose so that the people can satisfy their needs. The men hunt all day and yet there is no meat to show for their efforts. There is no happiness in the igloos, no oil to burn to give warmth and no meat to fill the children's bellies. The women are sad because they have no food for their children." All the while he kept carving on his wooden mask. He had already carved a number of little amulets in the shape of seals and two small thumb less hands, which he would be attaching to the mask. Also feathers were nearby and ready to be attached.

The kids understand the status of the shaman and his duties to his people. To carry out his duties he needed help from the Inuas, the spiritual occupants of all living and inanimate things. These in turn would help the shaman complete his tasks, he called them spirit helpers. All Inuas possess a human face but only rarely is it ever revealed.

To further complete his tasks the shaman is at times in need of face masks or masks as big as a man. These masks were usually made by the shaman himself or by a skilled craftsman under the direction of the shaman. Wood was mainly used for their construction with feathers or small carvings attached to it. The masks were often used only for a single performance or ceremony and then tossed, as it was believed that their powers were spent after being used. Some of the masks have broad beneficial powers, while others were made for a specific purpose and often discarded after use, as their powers would be depleted. Each mask derived its powers directly from the thing it represented and therefore was usually made in its image. No two masks were ever alike; the shaman would design them on an impulse or an inspiration. When the shaman wore the mask it was believed that the spirit dwelt within him, giving him special powers. These colourful and imaginative masks represented the powerful deities believed to control natural phenomena or the spirits of animals and other creatures.

"What can we do?" asked Amy.

"When I am finished with the mask I will summon the villagers to the meeting house and using the mask I will ask the deities for forgiveness for our sins. When the dance is finished we will journey to find Sedna and beseech her to free the animals," Tagak replied.

"Have you consulted with the Tungat to see why the animals are not available to the hunters?" Amy inquired.

"Yes, only yesterday I journeyed to the moon to plea to the Tungat, they wouldn't hear me. I confessed the sins of the people and begged the Tungat to release the animals but my pleas fell on deaf ears. On my return I stopped and talked to The Old One. He told me about you and said that you have powerful medicine and you would help me. That's why I sent my spirit helpers to find you. There, I have finished the mask; now it is time to begin," Tagak said, as he stepped back and inspected his handiwork.

Amy noted the mask looked like a bloated grotesque figure resembling a human face. There were two eyes, a nose and a mouth visible on the mask, with a hole in the forehead. The mouth was large and smiling with many large teeth. Two little thumb less hands were attached on either side of the mask. Around the hole in the forehead were attached little amulets of seals. The thumb less hands and hole in the forehead showed the willingness of The People to allow the animals to slip unmolested in and out of the domain of the Inuit. Tagak had used charcoal to colour a black band across the eyes to show that the deities see all and man was in the darkness when it came to the deities' powers. The smiling red mouth showed the happiness of the Inuit when they are allowed to feast on the animals, which give life to their village.

A thin black line of charcoal was drawn between the nose and mouth to show the separation of the air from the sea. For the mouth eats all creatures supplied by Sedna, the mother of all living creatures. The nose breathes the air supplied by Sila the air goddess. For the two could not be mixed. The feathers showed the freedom the animals would enjoy while in the land of The People.

Amy considered the thought and care that had gone into making the mask and felt that Sedna would truly be honoured by the labours of the old shaman. If only they were able to get to her before it is too late to save the starving villagers.

Tagak sent his assistant to assemble the villagers in the meetinghouse. Tagak and the Trapps proceeded to the meetinghouse to prepare for the dance. When all were assembled Tagak started the sacred chants of the shaman accompanied by his assistant on the drum. As Tagak danced wearing the mask he called on the spirits of his friends and relatives dead and alive to come to his assistance to persuade Sedna to free the seals. He made promises to the Tungat and to Sedna that proper respect would be shown by every villager to the animals if they were made available to the village's hunters. He told Sedna that he was bringing a respected and very powerful shaman with him when he visits her.

He hoped that this would please her and the new shaman would win her favour. Tagak knew that the deities respected powerful shamans and it always enhanced one's position to have powerful friends.

"*AIIIEEE,*" the eerie chant of Tagak shattered the silence and echoed across the land. Methodically Tagak's assistant beat the drum, boom-boom-boom, as he called out to his spirits.

Amy, Ty and Parker joined Tagak in his cry for assistance from the spirits. Their cries echoed across the land as they pleaded for guidance and strength to complete their journey. "*AIIIEEE,*" they chanted as the drum went boom-boom-boom.

Suddenly Tagak stopped dancing, he took off his mask and flung it into the fire, the dance had ended as suddenly as it had started.

"*Why did you throw your mask in the fire?*" Ty demanded to know.

"*Yeah, I thought it was neat. We could have taken it home if you didn't want it any more,*" Parker informed Tagak.

"*Now that the ritual is over, the spirits no longer dwell in the mask. It has to be destroyed lest it be inhabited by a Tarrak. You should know this!*" Tagak remarked looking suspiciously at the kids.

"*All masks are not destroyed after they are used,*" Amy declared.

23

"That's true, you are right. Some shamans do not destroy their masks but I destroy all masks after I have used them," Tagak boasted.

The assistant continued to methodically beat the drum while Tagak called on his friends' and families' spirits to help him find the way to Sedna. *"AIIIEEE,"* Tagak chanted, *"Come to me and help me on my journey,"* he cried, *"keep me strong, lend me your inyusuq* (the powerful forces that reside within individuals and serve as the source of good health, stamina, will power, and energy — all elements that give a person life), *to drive out the evil spirits,* (healthy friends and relatives would give their inyusuq to a sick person), *let me share your knowledge."*

The Trapps found themselves calling to their friends and relatives to lend them their inyusuq to assist them on the journey they would be taking with Tagak.

The villagers sitting in the meetinghouse encouraged Tagak and the Trapps to be strong during their journey. They called on the spirits to show them the way and protect them.

Amy looked at the assistant who was beating the drum. 'That's odd,' she thought. 'This drum has a seal for a handle.' Other drums she had seen had a human shape for a handle. The methodical beat of the drum was inducing a trance-like state. Boom-boom-boom, went the drum.

Above the chanting in the meetinghouse they heard Tagak cry, *"I see the way, it is starting to open up, we must follow the road-of-darkness to find Sedna."*

The villagers cried, *"Be brave and strong on your journey, return to us for we will be waiting."*

Once again the Trapps had the feeling that they were falling through the drum to begin their journey. Amy likened the feeling to diving into a lake.

chapter iii

the road-of-darkness

The Road-Of-Darkness, as the Trapps are about to learn, is not in total darkness. There are moments when the darkness is laid bare to the stark facts of life. Trials they will encounter will bring them back to the blazing reality of daily life. To toil in darkness is to be blind to reality. What awaits them on the road? The joy and terror, trials and tribulations that lay in wait will have to be met head-on and resolved. The seasons of the year are of

26

no concern to the road, it does not favour one season over the other. Each bend in the road can bring a change in the weather or a complete change of season.

Amy, Ty, Parker and Tagak will soon learn that all things are not as one-dimensional as they at first appear to be. This is not just a famine affecting The People but a famine that lies heavy upon the land like a plague. The very ecosystem of The People is being threatened to its core. Everything is affected and dying. Whatever has to be done to correct this disaster has to be done quickly. Can they correct the trespasses that have earned the scorn of Sedna? Are they up to the challenge?

Their odyssey began with the Trapps and Tagak winding their way down the road-of-darkness. 'Where will this road lead,' Amy wondered as they carefully crept along, because the road could not be seen. Their spirit helpers told them to take care as their footing could be suspect and they might fall into an abyss. They were also warned to be on the lookout for a Tarrak who could be lurking in the darkness to do them harm. If a dead person's relatives did not observe certain taboos, the dead person's soul became a dark, angry, enraged and malicious spirit. This spirit was known as a Tarrak or a Personal Shade and it haunted the area where the person died.

Tagak asked his spirit helpers to guide him and the young Kabloonas as they walked down the road of darkness, for they could easily lose their footing as they descended into the canyon down the narrow path to where Sedna resides.

"Amy, why don't you ask the light deity to light up this road, so that we can see where we're walking? It would be nice to see what we're tripping over," Parker asked his sister.

"Yeah, Amy that's a good idea, ask the light deities for some light. I for one am tired of tripping over all this stuff we can't see. We're going to have skinned knees or sprained ankles if this keeps up," Ty echoed the sentiments of his brother, as he stumbled along.

"It's worth a try," Amy replied. But try as she might the deities would not respond. *"Tagak, why won't the light deities reply?"* Amy queried.

"I don't know for sure, but I don't think they have any control over the Road-Of-Darkness. Whatever obstacles exist on the road have to be met head-on and overcome. The deities cannot interfere with the conditions as they exist," Tagak replied.

"I see, so we're stuck with whatever comes up," Ty remarked.

"*I'm afraid that is the way it is and the way it has to be,*" Tagak responded.

"*That's just great, we're stuck in something we have no control over again,*" Ty cried, as the group trudged wearily along the darkened road.

the howling

Navigating the road with all its obstacles was tough on the travellers. After walking and stumbling in the darkness for a great distance the group heard something coming towards them.

"Listen! What's making that noise?" Amy asked, to no one in particular, as she strained her ears to catch the muffled sound growing louder by the minute.

"I don't know," stated Tagak as he focused his attention on the noise.

Ty and Parker listened and shook their heads, they didn't know.

The sound grew louder and the bloodcurdling screams and the howling the creature was making sent shivers up and down their spines.

"Aaaarrrrgh," came the screams out of the darkness.

"Jiminy-Willie-Peppers what's that?" Parker cried as his hair stood on end and his eyes grew round as saucers.

"Whatever it is, it sounds like it's in a lot of pain and it's out for revenge on whoever caused its suffering," Amy replied with a quivering voice.

"It sounds like a Tarrak," Tagak whispered with fear in his voice, as he peered into the black hole ahead.

A form started to take shape and emerge from the darkness, dimly at first and then it was before them in solid form.

"I don't like the looks of this! Look how ugly it is! I've never seen anything that ugly in my whole life," Ty howled as he started to back up while staring at the creature coming towards them.

"Stay close. We must not show fear and we have to stand our ground!" Amy shouted with not much confidence in her voice. "We cannot be deterred from our mission."

"We should have brought the amulet with us, Amy. We're in a lot of trouble," Ty yelled to Amy.

"I know we should have, Ty, but we didn't have it with us when we were summoned and there's nothing we can do about it now. We're just going to have to do without it," Amy replied to Ty.

"It's okay Amy, we'll get along without the amulet. We'll just have to use our shamanistic powers," Parker reminded his sister.

"You're right Parker, we'll have to make do with what we have," Amy responded, trying to sound brave in the face of mounting danger.

The group could see the Tarrak was a malicious black ugly soul with revenge in its huge, red bloodshot eyes. The eyeballs were just floating in the eye sockets. There were no eyelids and the eyes bounced and rolled around with the Tarrak's antics. The Tarrak was grotesque in appearance; its head was huge and misshapen, with long black straggly hair blowing in the wind. The mouth was overly large with huge crooked black teeth protruding beyond the giant red lips that were covered with spittle. The nose was something else. Not only was it huge in comparison to the large head, it was bent over pulling the nose up and exposing the two nostril openings. From its appearance a person would expect to see smoke or fire pouring out of the openings. One arm appeared to be a wing with claws instead of fingers. The other had an overly large front leg of a polar bear with huge walrus tusks protruding from the paw where claws should have been. The left leg appeared to be human although grossly out of shape with a caribou hoof where a foot should be. The right one was in the shape of a seal with a human foot where the rear flippers should have been. The body was a tangled torso which was twisted at odd angles. They could see right away that it meant to do them harm. It appeared bent on tearing them limb from limb, as it shrieked and flailed its arms and staggered about in a menacing manner.

It was a terrifying sight to behold; even the strongest of men would tremble from the sight the group had to endure. The scene before them was bad enough but the screams and antics they were forced to face made their blood run cold and scared the daylights out of them.

Parker was so scared from the sight of the Tarrak he thought he had lost his voice, his mouth was working but no sounds were coming out. When he found his voice he screamed, *"Run we haven't got a chance, he's going to kill us. Run for your life,"* he said as he started to turn to run.

"Wait! Do what I do!" yelled Amy, trying to muster as much confidence in her voice as she could because she was as terrified as the rest were.

Following Amy's lead Ty, Parker and Tagak held up their right hands and said, *"Stop! We are shamans on a mission. We have powerful medicine."*

The Tarrak stopped in its tracks. They faced off, eyeball to eyeball. It had never encountered anyone who would stand defiantly before it. The spittle was flying from its lips as the enormous head swung from side to side as it screamed and raged.

"Aaaarrrrgh," roared the Tarrak.

They should have been running for their lives with the Tarrak in hot pursuit. The Tarrak was confused. It had never faced anything that hadn't trembled with fear. They should be begging for leniency and praying to be spared the wrath of the Tarrak. Who were these intruders who dared to invade the space he occupied? The Tarrak came to realize it wasn't strong enough to overcome the shaman's medicine; it reluctantly turned and fled screaming and howling down the narrow road.

"Jiminy-Willie-Peppers that was close," Parker wailed.

"The sound of that Tarrak coming at us scared me; but I can't help feeling sorry for it. I hope someday it finds the peace it deserves," Amy stated.

Tagak just nodded his head and looked at the young shaman with renewed admiration. To fear something and yet show compassion towards it is a rare trait, not enjoyed by very many. All that Kadluk told him about the young shaman was true. Tagak was indeed fortunate to have them accompany him on this journey.

CHAPTER V

NANOOK IS HUNGRY

The group could hear him coming long before they could see him. In his own environment at times he is impossible to see, because his natural colouring blends so well with his surroundings. Even though they couldn't see him, they knew he was near. There is no mistaking the growl of the mighty Nanook. All creatures that live in the realm of Nanook fear and respect him for who he is, the Teacher who taught the Inuit to hunt and provide for themselves. He is fearless in his pursuit for food, nothing stands in his way. Anything that flies, walks or swims in the polar bear's domain is prey to him. Although his main diet consists of seal, his diet varies with the type of food that is at hand. He is indiscriminate and will eat anything he can find. The bear suddenly stood before them. They could see that he was half starved. His hide hung from his frame, unlike a healthy, well-fed bear that would be round and appear full. The bear stood on his hind legs and drew himself up to his full height. Swinging his head from side to side he clawed the air and growled. *"Grrrooowl,"* roared the mighty bear. He was gigantic and menacing in appearance. Even the bravest armed men tremble at the sight of a fully grown Nanook when he is aroused. On his hind legs his growl which started deep in his chest and rushed up to his throat, burst upon the land. It could be heard by all those who could hear. The mighty Nanook would not be denied his rightful share of the bounty of the land. It told them he was about to dine on the very food that would allow him to survive and end his famine. His roar informed the other lesser predators that Nanook was going to eat and they too may attend the site and share in his bounty. The bear is not greedy and always leaves some of his feast for the less fortunate who are not as proficient at hunting as he is.

39

"Jiminy-Willie-Peppers," Parker howled, *"we've got to run! He's going to kill us."*

"Stand your ground!" cried Amy. *"Kadluk told us we have to be brave, we can't be brave by running away. Besides, I don't think we can outrun him."*

"We don't have the amulet to protect us and we don't have any weapons," wailed Ty. *"What would you propose we hold our ground with. I'm with Parker, I think we should run and hope for the best."*

"We can't outrun him! Spread out. Maybe we can appear bigger to him and he will think twice about attacking us. It is quite obvious that he is weak from hunger. Look how his hide is hanging from his bones," Amy said to her brothers.

"I think his starved condition would be all the more reason for him to attack and eat us," observed Parker. *"We would be an easy meal for him because we are defenceless."*

"Take the stance, like Kadluk showed us, remember we are the shaman!" Amy shouted to her brothers and Tagak, as she took an aggressive stance and faced the menacing bear.

Nanook couldn't believe his eyes. Before him stood four unarmed people. Not since last year during the annual migration which took him past the Churchill dump had he been so fortunate. Fortune was certainly shining on him today just as it had last year when a hunter who had taken more caribou than he could use had disposed of the five caribou carcasses at the dump. It had taken him two full days of casual eating to consume the five caribou carcasses. He could feel the same satisfaction now as he felt when he first observed the caribou carcasses and he welcomed the opportunity to leisurely consume the banquet that now stood before him. He began to drool and grunt with satisfaction knowing the sight before him would bring him a full belly. Surely the famine was over for him, or so he thought.

Suddenly an Inuit appeared between the group and the bear. The Inuit faced the bear. He, too, appeared to be unarmed. Although unarmed, the newcomer did not appear to fear the bear and he took the stance of the shaman when he was about to summon his powers. The Inuit appeared to be familiar but with his back to the kids they did not recognize him.

41

"Who is that and where did he come from?" Amy asked her brothers.

"Jiminy-Willie-Peppers! I don't know but I'm sure glad to see him, whoever he is," exclaimed Parker.

"I hope it's Kadluk. He's the only one I know who would have a chance of getting us out of this mess!" howled Ty.

Then they heard the familiar voice as it spoke to Nanook's Inua.

"Why do you stalk my young friends?" Kadluk asked the bear.

"All who live in my world are food to me!" declared the bear.

"You will not harm the young Kabloonas!" Kadluk stated.

"Who denies me my right to food?" The bear demanded.

"I do!" Kadluk snapped.

"Then, you too will be part of my meal! You have no weapons to stop me," the bear grunted with satisfaction.

"I need no weapon to stop you!" Kadluk stated as a matter of fact.

The polar bear hesitated. He had never before encountered an Inuit who possessed the confidence that this Inuit was displaying. What Inuit in his right mind would be so foolish as to stand before the

42

mighty Nanook unarmed and challenge him? Nanook was already thinking how lucky he was to have such a feast presented to him and he didn't even have to work for it. He started to drool as he took a step closer to the tasty meal before him. Something was wrong. This Inuit was not like any he had encountered before. He did not fear Nanook like he should. The bear stopped and stared at Kadluk while shaking his head and roared, *"Grroowl,"* which echoed across the land. The very ice they stood on shook from the mighty roar. Nothing happened. The bear took a step backwards for he remembered the other bears' talk of an Inuit who stood bare handed before a full grown Nanook. What name did that Inuit go by? Try as he might, the bear couldn't remember. Could this possibly be the same Inuit? The bear felt his chances of having a good meal disappear. That bear was in good health and was beaten. The bear didn't like his chances. If he lost the fight would he have enough strength to continue? On the other hand, if he won, he would have enough food to possibly carry him through the famine. He must know the name of the one who defies him before he makes up his mind. *"By what name are you known?"* the bear asked Kadluk.

"I am known as Kadluk by some and as THE OLD ONE by others!" Kadluk informed the bear.

The bear searched his memory. Why were these names familiar to him? Then it all came rushing back and a shutter ran the length of his body as he realized who he was facing. The one who long ago had faced the full grown polar bear was named Kadluk and he later was known as THE OLD ONE. Even among the bears THE OLD ONE was a legend because his feats were immeasurable. Everyone knows if you know what's good for you, you leave THE OLD ONE alone. The bear thought a long time about his chances of winning a fight. To destroy a legend would surely enhance the bear's stature, but could he win? Only a fool enters a fight if he is not sure of winning.

"I only stalked the Kabloonas because I am starving, I meant them no harm," the bear told Kadluk.

"You are not the only one who is starving! There is a famine across the land. Everything is starving. The young Kabloonas are on a quest to find out why we are suffering the wrath of Sedna. Tagak, the shaman who travels with the Kabloonas, has already visited the Tungat but they will not speak to him. They must be unharmed to continue on their journey or we will all perish," Kadluk informed the bear.

The bear knew he was beaten before the fight had a chance to start. Even if he won the fight he would lose for he would destroy the only chance the

44

land had to end the famine. He was glad he had asked the Inuit his name before he attacked. The bear had never before met Kadluk but he looked him over real good and sized him up, should they ever encounter each other again. With a grunt the huge bear spun on his hind legs, dropped to the ground and walked swiftly towards the leading edge of the fast ice. Before diving into the frigid waters, the bear gave one quick glance over his right shoulder for one last look at the one they call THE OLD ONE. He dove into the water and quickly disappeared beneath the waves searching for the food that wasn't there.

As the bear vanished so did Kadluk and the little group was again left to continue on its quest to find Sedna.

"Jiminy-Willie-Peppers, where did Kadluk go? I was watching the bear disappear beneath the water and when I looked back, Kadluk was gone," Parker cried in disbelief.

"I don't know I didn't see him go either. He must have something else to do that's important," Amy replied to her brother.

chapter vi

ukpik starves

Rounding a corner on the Road-Of-Darkness, the beautiful Ukpik came into view. It was standing on a knoll off to the right of the road.

Parker was the first to see the Snowy Owl. *"Jiminy-Willie-Peppers!"* he exclaimed, *"What's wrong with that bird?"*

"What do you mean?" Amy asked as she viewed the bird before them.

"Look at its feathers. They're dull looking. The other owls we've seen have a beautiful sheen to them," Parker stated.

"Yes, you're right, it looks sick," Amy observed.

"I'll say it looks sick. Look at its eyes. They should be big and full of life," Ty remarked.

"You're right! Its big beautiful yellow eyes appear to be dull and vacant," Amy said as she closely looked at the once-magnificent raptor.

The mighty night hunter most feared by birds and small rodents alike now appears to be as vulnerable as the game it preys on. It stands on the knoll staring at the tundra that surrounds it. Its vacant eyes search endlessly for what it cannot see.

"What is wrong with it, Amy?" Parker asked his sister.

"I don't know. I don't know anything about owls!" Amy replied.

"Well, ask it, Amy. Ask it what is wrong," Parker howled.

"Mr. Owl, is there something wrong? You don't look well!" Amy asked of the owl.

"I am hungry, I haven't eaten in days. I can't find any food. What is happening to the land?" Ukpik wanted to know.

"A famine has struck the land and everything is starving," Amy advised the bird.

"Do you have any food I can eat?" the owl asked.

"No, we have no food," Amy replied.

"Why do you travel the Road-Of-Darkness?" the owl inquired.

"We are on a mission to speak to Sedna and find out why the famine has struck the land. We will speak for the people and confess their sins. We will ask Sedna to again bring harmony to the land, so that the people can again enjoy its bounty," Amy told the owl.

"Then you must hurry. We cannot last much longer if these conditions persist," the once-magnificent bird replied as he bid them farewell and a safe journey.

The group continued on their way, leaving the emaciated bird to once again continue his search for the food he would never find.

chapter vii

tuktu digs

It wasn't getting any easier on the group. Stumbling along in the darkness is not a comfortable way to travel. One can easily fall or just as likely twist an ankle from a hole in the ground or from stepping on an unseen object lying on the road. In winter, walking on packed snow or an icy surface can be disastrous to the unsuspecting when your feet suddenly shoot from under you and your body is slammed onto the ground you once stood on.

"Look ahead, there's snow on the ground," Amy cried in disbelief.

50

"*What are we getting into now?*" Ty wailed as he peered ahead.

"*Jiminy-Willie-Peppers, it's turning into winter!*" Parker shouted.

Tagak never said anything. He looked ahead and saw the snow which covered the road. A change of seasons never bothered Tagak. He learned long ago you could not change the seasons so you just learned to live with them as they changed. It mattered not whether it was summer or winter, for both had their advantages and their drawbacks.

Drawing nearer to the corner they could see the ground was covered in snow for a great distance.

"*I don't like the looks of this, this could get nasty,*" Ty informed the group.

"*Don't be so pessimistic,*" Amy chided Ty.

"*Yeah it will be okay, won't it Amy?*" Parker asked in a questioning voice.

"*I'm sure it will, Parker. We just have to see what's up ahead,*" Amy reassured her little brother.

Tagak stopped walking and stared straight ahead.

"*What's the matter Tagak? What do you see?*" Amy shouted.

"*It's a caribou! What is it doing?*" Parker cried.

51

"It looks like it's trying to scrape the snow or ice away," Tagak informed the kids.

"Why would it be trying to do that?" Amy queried.

"It has to get the snow and ice off the lichens so that it can eat them," Tagak stated.

"He doesn't look very good, he looks pretty emaciated," Ty commented while looking at the caribou.

"There must be something wrong with it. Normally it would never let us get this close. It would have run away by now," Tagak advised.

"Mr. Caribou, what are you doing?" Amy asked in an inquiring voice.

"I'm trying to get this ice off the lichens. I'm starving and I can't get any food," the caribou remarked.

"Why can't you get the ice off the lichens?" Parker queried.

"The ice is too thick, my hoofs are sharp and they can break through most ice, but this ice is too thick. I can see the lichens but I can't reach them. Can you help me?" asked the caribou.

"Can we help him?" Amy asked Tagak.

"I don't see how. We have nothing that will break through ice that thick," Tagak replied.

"We can help him by getting Sedna to end the famine," Parker blurted out.

"I think you're right, Parker. The only way to help any of these animals is to get Sedna to end the famine. We must hurry. We have no time to lose," Amy advised her group.

netsik searches

"Will this road never end?" Ty muttered as he trudged down the seemingly never ending road.

"I see open water ahead!" Amy cried out as she pointed her finger at the water that appeared to be a brilliant blue in the distance.

"Jiminy-Willie-Peppers, what's that laying on the fast ice?" Parker howled.

"It looks like a Netsik," Tagak informed the group.

"What's a Netsik? I've never heard of a Netsik," Amy asked Tagak.

"It's a ringed seal. It is known by a lot of different names, but I know it as a Netsik," Tagak replied.

"What's it doing?" Ty asked.

"Nothing, by the looks of it. It's just lying on the ice. Seals are usually plump and full. It looks awful thin, to me," Amy shrugged.

"It appears the famine has affected the seals' habitat also," Parker observed.

As the group neared the seal they could see that it was too weak to even lift its head from the fast ice. The glassy eyes of the seal fixed on the group as they approached. The emaciated condition of the seal was evident. It did not possess the strength to even attempt to escape the approach of the group. It was too weak to move.

"What has happened to you?" Amy asked the seal.

"I can't catch any food. I tried and tried but I'm unable to catch anything that I can eat. With my last strength I managed to pull myself onto the ice so that I wouldn't drown. I have no strength left. What will become of me?" the seal asked.

"What food were you trying to catch?" Parker wanted to know.

"I tried to catch my favourite, the arctic cod, but

56

I couldn't find any. I couldn't even find the usually plentiful crustaceans or the krill I like to eat. Where has everything gone?" the seal pleaded.

"A famine has hit the land. We are on a quest to find Sedna and confess the sins of the people and beg her forgiveness, so that harmony may once again embrace the land," Amy told the seal.

"Hurry, we cannot last long," the seal replied.

"Be careful, do not go near the edge of the fast ice, it does not look solid," Tagak warned the kids.

"Where is this road going to lead us next?" Ty wanted to know.

"There is a lot of suffering on the land, we do not have any time to waste, we must hurry to our final destination," Amy advised her group.

"And where would that be?" Ty demanded to know.

"It's wherever this road leads us, isn't it Amy? Sedna will be at the end of this road!" Parker offered with enthusiasm.

"Yes Parker, Sedna should be at the end of this road if Tagak's vision is correct," Amy replied.

"You mean it might not be correct?" Ty howled.

"I didn't say that! Tagak has seen this road in his vision and said this is the road we must take to get to Sedna's house," Amy sternly advised Ty.

57

"That is right, Amy, this is the road I've seen, this is the road we must take," Tagak added.

"Let's get going, we're wasting time," Amy said as she turned and continued down the Road-Of-Darkness.

The road had turned into a narrow ribbon of ice as it meandered across the open water and disappeared out of sight. The road was strewn with rocks, pieces of caribou antler and other things that had been discarded over time. The group continued to walk around the items and sometimes tripped over them. These are the obstacles they encountered when the road was in darkness. The debris hindered their progress and caused them to trip and lose their footing as they travelled the road.

Tagak walked close to the edge of the road to avoid the debris in his path. *"Lookout! Help me!"* screamed Tagak, as his feet slipped on the ice and he slid off the edge of the road. His arms were flailing the air and his hands grasped in vain trying to find something that would prevent him from the fate that was inevitable. His thrashing feet entered the water and soon he was bobbing like a cork in the frigid waters. Although his body shot into the water like an arrow his shoulders and head never went below the surface.

Ty, who was closest to Tagak, without

thinking and without regard for his own safety, reached out and grabbed Tagak by the hood of his parka. *"Help me!"* Ty yelled to Amy and Parker as he put his arm out for them to grab while keeping a firm grip on Tagak's parka.

"How come Tagak never sunk below the surface of the water when he fell in?" Amy asked.

"It's because his parka is made of caribou hide," Parker answered.

"What do you mean by that, what has that got to do with it?" Amy wanted to know.

"Caribou hair is hollow and therefore it's a good insulator for warmth and acts like a cork because of the trapped air in the hollow follicles," Parker advised her.

"Is that right, Tagak, is what Parker said true?" Amy queried.

"Yes, Amy, what Parker said is true," Tagak replied as the kids pulled him on to the narrow roadway.

With the problem of getting Tagak out of the water solved, another and just as serious problem reared its ugly head. The water that clung to Tagak's clothes froze as soon as the clothes broke the surface of the water. Tagak was turned into a giant icicle. His clothes were a huge chunk of ice.

"Tagak looks like a huge icicle," Ty said to no one in particular as he stared at Tagak.

"You're right, he does," laughed Parker.

"This is no laughing matter," Amy scolded her brothers.

"Quick you have to get this ice off me," Tagak shouted.

"How do we do that?" cried Amy.

"Use a piece of caribou antler and that walrus tusk," Tagak wailed as he nodded towards the items lying on the road.

"What good will that do?" Ty howled.

"You can use them as beating sticks and break the ice from my clothing," Tagak informed the kids.

"It's about time this stuff we're tripping over, became of some use to us," Parker observed as the kids picked up the pieces of antler and tusk and began beating on Tagak's clothing. This caused the ice that clung to the clothing to shatter into millions of ice particles and fall from Tagak's clothes.

The potentially fatal tragedy that had befallen the little group was soon a distant memory as they once again continued their trek down the Road-Of-Darkness. They would not have the luxury of dwelling on the incident because it was imperative that they continue towards their common goal. A far more serious tragedy awaits them if they fail to complete their mission successfully. No second chances would be given for failure.

chapter ix

the old woman

The road had been a long exhausting trek with lots of pitfalls. Despite the hardships they finally reached the canyon floor. In the distance Sedna's house could be seen standing on a knoll. Between them and the house they could see a wall being erected, by the old woman who guarded the Road-Of-Darkness to Sedna's house.

"Who is that old woman and why is she building that wall?" Ty asked as he looked towards the old woman.

"*She's the old woman who guards the Road-Of-Darkness to Sedna's house,*" Tagak informed the kids.

"*Well, why does she need a wall? There's nothing here,*" Parker observed.

"*She doesn't want us to get to Sedna's house,*" Tagak advised.

"*Why doesn't she want us to see Sedna?*" Amy queried.

"*Kadluk said the old woman might try to bar our path to Sedna!*" Tagak informed the kids.

"*And you didn't think that was important enough to tell us before? Haven't we endured enough on this road already? What else did Kadluk tell you?*" Ty demanded of Tagak.

"*He said if the old woman was building a wall, we would have to stop her before she completed it or we wouldn't be able to see Sedna,*" Tagak stated.

"*Jiminy-Willie-Peppers, how are we going to stop her?*" Parker shouted.

"*Hurry,*" said Amy, "*we must knock the wall down before she's finished, we must not be denied access to Sedna. Sedna must really be angry with The People, if she is letting the old woman bar us from her house.*"

"*What do you think The People could have done that would make Sedna so angry?*" asked Parker.

"*I have no idea what could have happened, and we'll probably never know. All we can do is ask for forgiveness and try to make sure it never happens again,"* Amy told the group.

"How can we do that when we don't know what was wrong in the first place?" Ty pleaded.

"We can do it by showing the proper respect to all things in the future like we're supposed to," Amy advised the group.

"Jiminy-Willie-Peppers, we better stop talking and start doing something, she's building that wall really fast," Parker shouted.

"How do we knock the wall down? What should we use, we have no tools?" Tagak inquired.

"The only way it can be knocked down is with our shoulders," Amy informed the group.

"How do you know that?" Ty demanded an answer.

"I just know it. Come quickly, we don't have any time to lose!" Amy snapped at her brother.

The Trapps and Tagak ran at the wall and using their shoulders like a battering ram they threw themselves against the wall. Upon impact the wall crumbled from their combined assault. The old woman seeing the wall collapse quickly fled, for she knew she was not strong enough to confront the powers of these shamans.

chapter x

the end is near

The way was now open to the house of Sedna.

Cautiously they approached the house and knocked on the door. A shrill voice bade them enter. Upon opening the door they observed a dirty, dishevelled old woman with matted hair, sitting in a chair with her back to them.

"Sedna is very distraught with what has happened — look at her unsightly appearance. See! There to her right she has penned up all the animals. That is why none are roaming in the realm of the Inuit," Amy stated.

To the right of Sedna was a locked pen where the land animals were walking in circles, unable to get free. Beside this pen was a pool where all the sea creatures were swimming in circles and beside the pool was a cage which contained all the birds that fly in the sky.

"Look up!" Ty said pointing skyward, *"The house has no roof."*

"That is because Sedna wants to see everything that goes on and would be unable to keep an eye on everything if a roof blocked her view," Tagak informed the group.

"Be quick now," Amy said to Tagak. *"I'll comb her hair with my fingers and clean her up while you confess the sins of The People and ask for forgiveness. Ty, you and Parker straighten up her house."*

While Tagak confessed The Peoples' sins and begged for forgiveness, he told Sedna how the villagers were suffering because of the animals not being available for them to hunt. He feared for their very survival if Sedna did not show them favor and release the animals.

Tagak confessed for the sins of The People and promised Sedna that The People would conform to the laws of the land in future and show the proper respect that was required to maintain harmony in the land. He promised Sedna all this and prayed she could see fit to release the animals and end the famine that was plaguing the land. He reminded Sedna that the people and all living things were in danger of vanishing if the famine continued. Amy, who was combing Sedna's hair with her fingers and washing her face, was trying to give Sedna the feeling of wellbeing that only comes from a thorough cleansing of the body and soul. Ty and Parker busied themselves straightening up the sparse furnishings in Sedna's dwelling but with no effect. It soon became apparent they were getting nowhere.

"What is wrong, why isn't Sedna responding?" Parker inquired.

"I don't know, Parker. We're doing everything we can but nothing seems to be working," Amy replied.

Suddenly where nothing had been before, now stood Kadluk. He approached Sedna and spoke softly in her ear. A smile appeared and grew on Sedna's face as she nodded her head.

"Kadluk, how did you get here?" Amy demanded to know.

Ty, Parker and Tagak were too flabbergasted to speak. They just stood and stared at THE OLD ONE. They couldn't believe what they were seeing.

"It matters not," was Kadluk's reply to Amy.

"Sedna was not responding to us. How did you get her to smile and nod her head?" Amy asked.

"She said she would have responded to you but she was enjoying your company and the attention she was getting from you. She said it is not often you visit and she enjoys your company," Kadluk advised Amy.

"Why did she respond to you so fast?" Amy wanted to know.

"I just reminded her, The People and all things are starving and the problem needed her immediate attention. Time is of the essence. I reminded her of the hardships you encountered on your trip to see her. You showed great respect by never deviating from your quest and continuing your trek even though you suffered many personal hardships. I reminded her that you did it for The People and not for any personal gain. Sedna has respect for those who think of others instead of themselves when hardship befalls the land," Kadluk informed Amy.

"Boy, are we ever glad to see you, Kadluk. You won't believe what we've been through!" Ty shouted excitedly.

"Yeah, you should have seen the Tarrak. It terrified us. I thought it was going to kill us," Parker shouted as he trembled at the thought of the Tarrak as it menacingly stalked them.

"There will be time for relating your heroic deeds

at future feasts. Now is not the time. You still have much to do," Kadluk informed the boys, as he turned his attention to Amy, as she stood in front of Sedna.

Before their eyes they noticed a change taking place. It was apparent that Sedna was accepting the confessions from the old shaman and that she was benefiting from the personal grooming that Amy was administering to her. They saw the change in Sedna's demeanor, immediately, She was becoming happy with The People again, the lines of age quickly changed into the look of a mature woman, more befitting the mother of all things. It was plain to see that she was happy that the young shamans had seen fit to pay her a visit. Reaching down, she unlocked the pens and allowed the creatures to once again roam unmolested in the land of The People. Sedna advised the shaman that she would tell the Tungat to ensure there were sufficient animals for The People to harvest. The famine would end as quickly as it started. Harmony would once again come to the land of The People.

Tagak assured Sedna that the people would show proper respect to the animals in the future and there would be no further transgressions. Their meeting with Sedna was over; with harmony again restored upon the land, it was time to leave.

chapter xi

the feast

The group began the journey that would return them to the village and The People. Returning to the Road-Of-Darkness they found the obstacles that had been placed before them when they began their trek had been removed and they were free of the pitfalls that had befallen them in the beginning.

"This is a welcome sight, being able to see and not have to trip and stumble over all the debris that was on the road coming down. Now if we could just get

something to eat, I'm starving," Ty remarked.

"Yeah, this is easy to walk on. But please don't mention food. I'm so hungry my stomach thinks my throat has been cut," Parker added as he fell in beside his brother for the hike that lay ahead of them.

"Will you two cut it out, we're all hungry and you're just making it worse talking about food when we don't have any!" Amy admonished her brothers.

They walked in silence. Their energy was spent, the long journey and the lack of food and water was taking its toll. Luckily the road was now a pleasant walk and the group quickly travelled up the Road-Of-Darkness to the village. As they neared the village they could hear the sound of laughter and the joy of kids playing. When the group came into view of the village, the villagers became silent. The group had another member; they now had one more person than when they left. Kadluk had joined the group on its return trip. The villagers were suspicious and viewed the group with caution as it approached. The elders recognized Kadluk as he drew nearer. The younger villagers had never seen Kadluk. They only knew of him because the elders had sung his praises at many feasts. They only knew him as the shaman who could do things no other person could do. To them he was a legend, someone to look up to and emulate. They never in their wildest dreams ever dreamt they would live to see him in person. He was a person bigger than life. The elders quickly told the villagers they were being honoured by the presence of THE OLD ONE. One and all came running to see the legend enter their village.

"I can smell food from here," Ty howled as they entered the village.

The villagers recognized the starving state of their guests and quickly escorted the group to the feast that was underway. The ladies offered them the choicest cuts of meat as they were the guests of honor. There was no talking as the group dug into the food that was offered and their hunger was soon satisfied.

They had returned to much merriment upon their arrival and they had been greeted with the joy of hunters returning from hunting and reporting record numbers of animals being taken. There was a festive mood in the air and the group had the place of honour at the great feast. The villagers could be heard belching and passing gas in great quantities, the sign of a satisfying meal. Even the sled dogs were sleeping with bloated bellies with meat left untouched beside them, a further sign of the bounty the villagers were enjoying.

"Boy, I'm full," sighed Ty as he burped, undid his belt a notch and lay back on his arms.

"Leave it to you to be the first one finished," Amy remarked as she looked at her brother as he lounged on the ground.

"I'm full too, that was good," remarked Parker as he laid back and gave a contented sigh.

With the satisfaction of a full belly enjoyed by all, it was now time to be entertained by the re-enactments of past deeds. The villagers were indeed honoured to have Kadluk, the living legend and master story teller of his people, at this feast. There is no one alive who can re-enact a scene like Kadluk can. No story teller before him could act out a scene and keep his audience spell-bound like he could. He can move his audience to joy or to tears with a single gesture. When Kadluk entered the circle of the feast to extol the bravery of Tagak and the kids, he had the undivided attention of every villager. Not a noise was made, not even a whisper, as the villagers waited with anticipation of witnessing the greatest event that was about to unfold before their very eyes.

Kadluk started slowly relating to The People how and why Tagak and the Kabloonas had been called upon to undertake the treacherous journey to see Sedna and break the iron grip of the famine. The story unfolded as Kadluk used the movements of his arms and legs to emphasize certain parts of the story. A gasp of horror ran through the crowd as Kadluk re-enacted the terrifying encounter with the dreaded Tarrak, the vicious black ugly soul who was out to wreak havoc. In the face of certain annihilation they had stood their ground and stared down the deadly onslaught of the terrifying Tarrak. He took them to new heights as he acted out the encounter with the fully grown Nanook. He emphasized the courage the group displayed in the face of certain death when they encountered the starving bear. Nanook was bent on satisfying his hunger and nothing was going to deter him from his first meal in days. Kadluk took the villagers through the hardships the small group had to overcome to complete their task. Kadluk told the villagers they were fortunate to have Tagak as their shaman. He had shown much courage and vision to bring this tragedy to a happy ending.

It was with renewed admiration in their eyes the villagers now viewed the little group. They had not realized the dangers they had to overcome to complete their journey. The people were happy and boasted of Tagak's great strength and wisdom. His legend would grow.

Tagak knew he owed much to the young Kabloonas for the success of the odyssey they had all shared. He heaped praise on the young shaman, for without their help and knowledge he would not have been able to return the animals to The People and end the famine that had befallen the land. Tagak would relate this saga at many feasts in the years to come, ensuring The People never forgot the important role the kids played in restoring harmony to the land when all seemed lost.

*   *   *   THE END   *   *   *

GLOSSARY

Igloo - n, pl -*loos* a dome-shaped Inuit house, built of blocks of solid snow.

Inua - (inh'oo ah) n, the spiritual occupants, or spirit helpers, that reside in all living or inanimate things.

Inuit - The People

Inyusuq - (personal souls) n, the powerful forces that reside within individuals and serve as the source of good health, stamina, will power, and energy - all elements that gave a person life (to drive out evil spirits, healthy friends and relatives would give their inyusuq to a sick person).

Kabloona - White Man.

Nanook - Polar bear.

Netsik - Ringed seal (one of many names it was known by)

Sedna - a sea goddess who ruled over all the lesser spirits and monsters. She was considered to be the mother of both land and sea creatures and therefore the provider of all life.

Sila - an all-pervasive spirit which resides in the air.

Tarrak - a dark, angry, enraged and malicious spirit. If relatives did not adhere to certain taboos after a person's death the dead person's soul became enraged and malicious. This dark angry spirit was known to some Inuit as a personal shade or Tarrak.

Tuktu - Caribou

Tungat - (plural of tungak) the spirits who controlled the supply of game animals.

Ukpik - Snowy Owl.

The Author

Lawrence was born and raised in Alberta. 37 years of his adult life was spent serving in the Canadian Armed Forces and the Royal Canadian Mounted Police. The author draws on 10 years of living in the Yukon and the Northwest Territories for the inspiration for his stories. Retirement finds him again in Alberta where he presently lives with his wife Judith. They have 2 children and 6 grandchildren.

The Illustrator

Rob Adams, son of Lawrence Adams; when he is not working on his fathers illustrations, can be found working on game designs. Trained in Visual Communication, Rob currently works in the field of video games, juggling roles of a producer and game designer. Rob has had first hand experience of living and visiting many of the places described in the Trapps Family Adventure books.

Other books by Lawrence E.R. Adams.

the old one
the amulet
the stolen soul
the creator

Watch for future books by Lawrence
Adams as the Trapps Family Adventures continue
to explore the mysteries of the north.

the mine
who walks on my land
who swims in my waters
who flies in my skies
the spirit of marble island
the search for the red diamond
the little people
the rescue

Join Amy, Ty and Parker as they continue
to seek answers to life's adventures on the frozen
tundra.

GIVE A "**LAWRENCE E.R. ADAMS**" BOOK TO A FRIEND

Trapps Publishing
P.O. Box 212
Irricana, AB T0M 1B0
WWW.trappspublishing.com
Send to:

Name:_____

Street:_____

City:_____

Province/   Postal/
State:_____Zip Code_____

Please Send:

"THE OLD ONE"	_____	X @ $9.95 =_____
"THE AMULET"	_____	X @ $9.95 =_____
"THE STOLEN SOUL"	_____	X @ $9.95 =_____
"THE CREATOR "	_____	X @ $9.95 =_____
"THE FAMINE"	-------	X @ $9.95 =_____

Shipping and handling for first book @ $4.00
plus $1.00 each additional Book (Shipping and
handling free in Canada and Continental USA) =_____
5% GST =_____
Total amount enclosed: _____

Make cheque or money order payable to:
TRAPPS PUBLISHING
Price subject to change without prior notice.
ORDERS OUTSIDE OF CANADA must be paid in U.S. funds by cheque or money order drawn on U.S. or Canadian Bank.

Sorry no C.O.D.'s.